Collect them all!

You Decide   What Happens

GOD ALLOWS U-TURNS

YOUTH

GET Real!

WRITTEN BY

Allison Bottke and Heather Gemmen

ILLUSTRATED BY **Gary Locke**

Faith Builder

Ages 9 and up

Trust

A Faith Builder can be found on page 92.

FaithKidz®

Equipping Kids for Life

An Imprint of Cook Communications Ministries • Colorado Springs, CO

www.cookcommunications.com/kidz

Faith Kidz® is an imprint of Cook Communications Ministries
Colorado Springs, Colorado 80918
Cook Communications, Paris, Ontario
Kingsway Communications, Eastbourne, England

GET REAL!
©2004 by Heather Gemmen and Allison Bottke

First printing, 2004
Printed in the United States of America
1 2 3 4 5 6 7 8 9 10 Printing/Year 08 07 06 05 04

ISBN 0781439744

Designer: Granite Design

To my beautiful and precious daughter,
Mandy Bottke
May you continue to grow in your journey
as God shapes you into the amazing women
you are becoming. I love you.

−AGB

To Mikey and Elias Abeh,
You may think you have grown up,
but you'll never grow out of the place
you made for yourselves in my heart.

−HG

A special thanks goes to Vicki Caruana

who significantly helped shape this book.

Love does not delight in evil but rejoices with the truth. It always protects, always trusts, always hopes, always perseveres. Love never fails.

—1 Corinthians 13:6-8

This is a test!

You are the main character of this book. Your choices determine whether or not you are clapping in beat to your favorite band next to the cute new kid at your favorite concert or sulking by yourself at lunchtime.

Can you make it through middle school? Can you figure out how to handle friendships and faith, homework and home life without messing up? Better yet, can you make a U-turn when you *do* mess up?

Turn the page—if you dare.

GET Real!

The kitchen is littered with sandwich fixings. Your mom is furiously putting sandwiches together like she's about to feed an army!

"There are only five of us, Mom," you say.

"I know. I just want to make sure everyone has what they need," she says. Your mom is so cool to suggest that all your friends hang out at your house. She even paid for the movie rental!

The doorbell rings. This is going to be a blast. It's been awhile since all five of you have had time to just hang out. One thing or another got in your way. Between final exams, end of the semester projects, basketball season, and the school play, it's been pretty busy.

"I smell food!" C. J. says as he walks in the door and heads straight for the kitchen. He's always hungry!

"Make yourself at home," you say.

"Don't mind if we do," Craig says. "Man, it's been awhile since I've been here."

"Too long," Karen says. Karen is always the one with the cool head. She's not easily excited, but tonight she's downright giddy!

Charlene is the last to arrive and doesn't look too happy about it.

"Sorry I'm late," she says. "My big-shot big brother decided to make a few stops on our way here. I wish I had my driver's license!"

"Don't worry about it," you say. "You're here now. That's all that matters."

Charlene is the star player on the girls' basketball team. She helped take the team to regionals this year. She's been busier than the rest of your gang, which everyone calls Five Alive.

The five of you have known each other since kindergarten. Over the years you've had other friends, but you always drift back to these four. They know you better than anyone else. Now that all five of you are Christians, your friendship is on a whole new level.

Your mom serves the sandwiches and root beer. C. J. finds some chips hidden away in the pantry and adds them to the pile of food.

"A toast!" Karen suggests.

You all raise your frosty mugs.

"To us!" she says.

"To us!" the rest of you cheer.

Just then the phone rings. You wonder if it's Chris. You've known Chris for years, but just recently you noticed that Chris is kind of cute.

"It's for you," your mom says before handing you the phone.

"Who is it?" you ask.

"I don't know," she says and goes back to making a second batch of sandwiches.

"Turn that down!" you snap. C. J. mutes the movie and all of Five Alive watch you.

The phone conversation is over before it really begins. You didn't get to say one word. You drop

the phone to the ground and look to see if your mom is in earshot.

"Was it Chris?" Craig says, teasing you about your new crush.

"No. Couldn't really tell who it was," you say. "All the caller said was 'Five Alive better watch their step.'"

"Or what?" Craig asks.

"Or else," you say.

"What did we do?" C. J. asks. "Why would some-one threaten us like that?"

You're quiet. You know why. The caller did say it. It's just so unthinkable.

"What else did the caller say?" Karen asks. She could always see right through you.

"'You're not who you pretend to be. So cut the Christian act.'"

You search your brain trying to figure out what you or anyone else in Five Alive might have done that would make anyone think they were faking their faith. Nothing comes to you.

"Just forget about it," your mom says from behind you. You didn't know she was listening. "Whoever it was is obviously jealous of what you all have. Don't let it get to you."

If you listen to your mom, go to page 13.

If you spend the whole evening discussing the phone call, go to page 87.

"Yeah, my mom's right," you say. "We don't have any way to figure out who it is anyway."

"Okay, so the mystery is less about who called and more about why they called," Karen says. "Why would anyone accuse us of faking it?"

"Maybe because we don't always act like we're Christians," C. J. says quietly.

"Give me a break," Charlene says. "We're nice to everyone. What else are we supposed to do? Wear t-shirts?"

"Yeah, and we sure are good to each other," Craig says. "People don't know how you guys forgave me over that whole homework thing. No fake Christian would do that.

"Maybe that's it," says Karen. "Maybe we need to show others what we're like."

If you agree, go to page 15.

If you don't want to get any more attention for being a Christian, go to page 19.

You walk up to Mr. Mac's room with Five Alive the next week, ready for another Logos meeting. When you look in the classroom, you are shocked to see so many kids.

Go to page 22.

"You've got a point," your mom says. She is still listening. "I don't mean to keep interrupting. It just seems that whoever made that phone call either feels like you've hurt them or left them out somehow. Do you know anyone like that?"

You know that you haven't been very nice to Terry in recent weeks. But you haven't been mean.

"I think we need to be more visible," Karen suggests. "We're not the only Christians in the school."

"We could start a club for Christians," C. J. says.

"Yeah, but it should have a purpose—not just a social club," Charlene says.

"And not just to say we're Christians," Karen adds.

"What do you mean?" you ask.

"I mean that we need to invite others to be Christians."

"Oh," you say.

"We could have a prayer time before school once a week," Charlene suggests.

"Yeah," Karen says, her enthusiasm rising. "And we could help each other live as Christians."

"This sounds great," your mom says. "I'm impressed with you kids. However, it's unlikely that you'll be able to meet on campus unless you have a teacher who will sponsor your group or club."

"That's easy," Craig says. "Mr. Mac is a Christian. I'll bet he'd be willing to sponsor it."

That Monday, Five Alive meets with Mr. Mac after school, and he quickly agrees to sponsor your club—although he asks a pretty important question.

"What's your main reason for doing this?" he asks.

"We want to give kids a reason to gather together with a common belief," Karen says. She's always thinking—definitely the brainiac of Five Alive.

"We also want to take away any reason someone might have for calling us fakes and frauds," you say. The others look at you to shut up. They didn't intend to tell Mr. Mac about that disturbing phone call.

Thankfully Mr. Mac doesn't go down that road and goes to his desk. He searches through a pile of papers in his bottom drawer.

"Then I think this would fit your purpose nicely," he says and hands Karen a weathered sign. It says LOGOS in Greek lettering.

"This was the name of our club when I was in high school," Mr. Mac says. "It means *word* or *reason*. I've kept this, hoping someday to start it again where I taught. You guys are an answer to prayer for me."

That Friday morning before school, having publicized the Logos Club all week, Five Alive walks toward Mr. Mac's room.

No one is there except Mark. He's holding a paper in front of him and is reading it with wide eyes.

"Great, the only person who shows up is Mark," Craig whispers to you and Charlene.

"The Five Alive wanna-be," Charlene whispers back. "This ought to be fun."

You shrug, wondering if maybe your group really has been a little too exclusive.

"Guys!" Mark mumbles as you walk up to him. "Check this out. It was on the door."

Those who enter, prepare for battle. Get your Christian $#@ off campus!

While everyone else reacts with outrage and anger, you keep your eyes on the hallway thinking that whoever left this note is probably watching. Maybe making yourself more obvious as a Christian wasn't such a good idea.

If you go to the meeting, go to page 20.

If you don't go to the meeting, go to page 22.

"Why don't we forget about the phone call," you say. "It was probably just a prank anyway."

"I think we should deal with it," Karen says. "Not avoid it."

"Do what you want," you say. But you turn to C. J. and mutter, "Some kind of celebration this turned out to be."

You leave your friends in the kitchen and go back into the family room to watch the movie. After some whispering, your friends say their goodbyes and leave.

"Where did everybody go?" your mom asks.

"They were bored," you tell her. Privately, you hope they were bored of the conversation they were having.

But they obviously didn't stop talking about the phone call and its implications when they left your house. The next time you see them, they are still at it, trying to figure out how to make sure that people feel accepted by them.

If you give in and join the conversation, go to page 82.

If you don't join them, go to page 81.

C. J. pulls the note away from Mark just before Mr. Mac shows up to unlock the classroom. No one mentions the note to him.

Mr. Mac opens the meeting with prayer and then goes to the back of the room to work on his lesson plans. The six of you sit in silence. No one knows how to start or what to say.

"I know," Karen says. "If *logos* means **reason**, why don't we start by giving the reasons we want to meet?"

After a few minutes it's obvious that everyone came for different reasons. But one in particular both intrigues and scares you.

"I want a place where I can feel safe," Charlene says. "If I do something wrong, I want a place to come for help."

"You're safe here," Mark says. He's always had a little crush on Charlene.

"Is there something you need help with now?" Karen asks.

Without looking anyone in the eyes, Charlene blurts out, "I cheated on Mr. Ross's test."

You shoot a look back at Mr. Mac to make sure he isn't listening. He seems engrossed in his work.

"So what do we do now?" Craig asks.

"Forgive me," Charlene says. "And keep this secret for me. I'm trusting you guys."

The bell rings for first period and everyone rushes to their lockers in hopes of getting to class on time. Mark walks along with you since you both have math first period.

"Shouldn't we tell a teacher about Charlene?" he asks. "Charlene shouldn't be cheating."

If you ask Charlene to confess, go to page 83.

If you keep the secret, go to page 84.

If you tell on her, go to page 26.

If you go to Mr. Mac for advice, go to page 31.

"You know what?" you say. "I just remembered I can't come today."

"Why not?" Karen asks.

"There's something I have to do," you say without looking at her. "I'll catch up with you guys later."

You run out of the school before anyone can say anything else to you. Out in the schoolyard you lean against the building to catch your breath. Your heart pounds in your chest, but it's not from running—it's fear. The thought of going to that meeting scared you. It's a step you're not sure you're willing to take just now.

"Hey, haven't seen you around in a while," a familiar voice says.

"Terry, I didn't see you there," you say. That butterfly-in-your-stomach feeling about Terry is gone, but it doesn't mean you couldn't just hang out and talk for a while.

Better than being alone.

"Why aren't you inside with your real friends?" Terry says with obvious disdain.

"Don't feel like it," you say.

"Well, do you feel like shooting some hoops until the bell rings?" Terry offers.

"Yeah, I do!" you say.

You get to school early every day to play basketball with Terry. On Mondays you both watch as the rest of Five Alive and other Logos members enter the building for their meeting. Terry always has something to say to make fun of them, sometimes loud enough for them to hear, but mostly just to you. You ignore it at first, but as time goes by you find yourself laughing right along with Terry. Then there are days when Karen looks at you when Terry says something nasty. You know she doesn't understand why you are hanging around with Terry and not with them. You feel sad, but trying to live life their way seems way too hard.

If you go back to Logos, go to page 54.
If you don't go back, go to page 56.

The next morning you catch Charlene at her locker.

"We need to talk," you say. This isn't going to be easy.

"What's up?" she says while trying to cram her basketball uniform into her already full locker.

"You need to tell Mr. Ross you cheated on that test," you say. You close your eyes tight waiting for Charlene to explode.

She rests her head against her locker and then turns it to look your way. You open your eyes to see hers full of tears.

"I can't. I'm scared," she says.

"I'll come with you if you want," you offer. "It's the right thing to do, Charlene."

"If I tell, then I'll get a lower grade," she says.

"So?" you say. "You'll do better next time."

"You don't understand," she says. "I'll be kicked off the team. The state championship is next week. The team is counting on me."

This certainly puts a kink in things. Charlene is their star player. Everyone looks up to her. There's a lot of pressure on Charlene.

"Charlene, if we're going to be real about being Christians, we need to do the right thing even if it

hurts," you say. You know how hard this is for her. You've made the wrong choice more than once.

By this time Karen, C. J., Craig, and Mark have gathered at Charlene's locker. They are quiet, waiting to see what Charlene will do.

"I know you're right," she says. "Let me think about it for a while, though, before I do anything."

If you continue encouraging her to do the right thing, go to page 29.

If you tell on her, go to page 85.

If you go to Mr. Mac for advice, go to page 86.

"Yeah, cheating is pretty serious," you say.

"I think we should tell Mr. Ross," he says.

"Don't worry about it, Mark," you say. "I've been her friend a lot longer than you have. I'll take care of it."

"What are you going to do?" he asks.

"I'm going to tell Mr. Ross. Maybe he'll just make her redo the test and lose ten points or something. And then she won't dare do something like that again."

"Yeah. She'll probably end up being a pro basketball player someday. She can't get in the habit of cheating or she'll never make it through college."

"Right," you say. "We'd be lousy friends if we didn't do something."

You stand outside your English class at the end of the day waiting for everyone to leave. You and Charlene share this class, so it's not like you're talking to a teacher you don't know.

"Mr. Ross," you begin. "Do you have a minute?"

"Sure, what can I do for you today?" he says. Everyone likes Mr. Ross. He's one of the coolest teachers in the school.

"A friend of mine told me she cheated on our last English test," you say. "I don't want her to get into trouble, but she needs to come clean about it."

"Does this friend of yours have a name?" he asks.

"It's Charlene," you say. You thought you'd feel relieved, but you don't.

"Have you encouraged her to come forward?" Mr. Ross asks.

"Yes, but she refuses," you say. Suddenly you feel like a cat backed into a corner. You want to escape. "But I'll talk to her again."

"Sounds like we need to take more drastic action," Mr. Ross says. He punches the call button to the front office on the wall. "Ms. Taylor, could you call Charlene Rush's parents to come in for an emergency conference tomorrow morning?"

The garbled voice on the intercom confirmed Mr. Ross's request, and you stand there with your mouth hanging open. This didn't go the way you expected. You thought Mr. Ross was cool. Boy, were you wrong!

"Thank you for bringing this to my attention," he says. He walks you to the door and before closing it, says, "Let me know if you need anything else."

At your locker the next morning you keep a close eye on Mr. Ross's door. You know that Charlene and her parents are inside. It seems like they've been in there for hours! The bell rings and first period students stream into English. Charlene pushes through them and runs right into the girls' bathroom. Her parents walk arm in arm out of the building talking in whispers. You wish you were a fly on the wall of that classroom.

Even though the first bell rang, you stand outside the bathroom waiting for Charlene without looking like you're waiting for Charlene.

The door bursts open and Charlene runs right into you. As soon as she sees who it is, she bursts into tears.

"Someone squealed," she says. "Someone told Mr. Ross that I cheated. Who would do that? I only told people at Logos that day." She looks like she's about to scream. "Whoever did it must really hate me."

Charlene's eyes are all puffy and her new attempts at wearing makeup now make her look like a raccoon.

If you admit that it was you, go to page 66.

If you don't tell her it was you, go to page 67.

"The best thing to do is to be honest with your teacher, Charlene," you say. "It's not like you've done this before. It's a first offense."

"Do you think he'll let me redo the test?" Charlene asks.

"I don't know," Karen says. "There'll probably be a late penalty if you do."

"I don't know, guys," she says. "That's a big risk to take."

"It's a bigger risk to lie about it," C. J. says.

Over the next couple of days Charlene is incredibly busy practicing for the state finals with her team. Maybe she's avoiding all of you, since you don't even find an opportunity to talk to her after classes. You pray that she will do the right thing.

At the next Logos meeting, Charlene is absent. A strong sense of disappointment sweeps through the group. What does this mean? Has she totally blown

you all off? Has she turned away from what you all know is right? You know she's not sick, so where is she?

"I don't get it," Mark says. "Why did Charlene even confess to us if she doesn't want us to help her?"

"I think she's trying to sort things out," Craig says.

"Personally I think she's avoiding us," Mark says. His crush on her has turned to disappointment. "She's not who I thought she was."

If you believe in Charlene, go to page 33.

If you lose hope in Charlene, go to page 35.

"Don't worry," you say. "I'll take care of it." After all, you've known Charlene the longest. It's not Mark's place to say anything.

You stand outside the science classroom at the end of the day waiting for everyone to leave. You don't feel good about going straight to Mr. Ross about this. After all, it was his test she cheated on. And Mr. Mac has been such a great advisor to Logos; maybe he'll know what to do.

"Mr. Mac," you begin. "Do you have a minute?"

"Sure. How can I help?"

"A friend of mine confessed to me that she cheated on a test, and I thought you would know what I should do about it," you say while taking off your jacket. *When did it get so hot in here?*

Mr. Mac stops shoving papers long enough to look you straight in the eye.

"Well, if someone cheated on one of my tests, there would be nothing I could do about it unless she or he came forward or if I discovered it on my own. Anything you would tell me is slander," he says. "Besides, you're a little too old to be a tattle tale."

"Right," you say. "I don't want to tattle. But I do want to help her get back on track."

"So you don't want to tattle and you don't want to watch her continue making bad choices."

"Right. What should I do?"

"There's only one thing left to do."

"What?"

"I think you know."

"What? Talk to her? But she'd hate me!"

"You sound like someone who has a lot of compassion for your friend. I can see you have hope in her. I wouldn't hate you if you were my friend."

"But I'm afraid she will."

"Yes, sometimes it is scary to do the right thing. I'll be praying for you, okay?"

Mr. Mac stands silently in front of you for a while. There is nothing else to say, but you were hoping for an easier answer. Finally you thank him and walk away.

If you ask Charlene to confess, go to page 24.

If you don't talk to her, go to page 62.

"Mark, don't lose faith in Charlene," you say. "We all make mistakes. It's how we handle them that matters."

"But she isn't handling it at all!" Mark says.

"We don't know that," Karen says. "Give her some time."

After school you pass by the gym and see Charlene coming out of the locker room. She sees you and comes running toward you with a big smile on her face.

"Where were you this morning?" you ask. "We were worried about you."

"Don't be," she says. "I've taken care of everything."

You look at her with disbelief and say, "What's that supposed to mean?"

"It means I told Mr. Ross everything. I retook the test—with penalty of course. And I'm not kicked off the team!" Charlene is practically glowing with excitement.

"What did your coach say?" you ask.

"He announced during practice that I came forward and that he was rewarding my honesty. Can you believe it?" she says. "And I have detention tomorrow after school. I'll have to miss practice."

"Wow! That's amazing," you say. Who knew Coach K would reward anything? He always seemed so hard on kids.

You're lost in thought as you leave the school. Charlene is a different girl. She's happy. She's practically giddy. Then it hits you. She's free! Free from hiding what she did. What a difference!

"Hey!" a girl in your science class shouts from the bike racks. "Are you in Charlene's Logos Club?"

"Yeah," you say.

"Great! See you there on Monday," she says before riding off. This girl is on the basketball team with Charlene.

A half dozen kids you've never met come to the next Logos meeting. Even though you all planned this as an outreach to the rest of the students, you didn't expect it to grow so fast.

If you are excited to see others coming, go to 37.

If you don't want others to come, go to 39.

The next day you catch Charlene right before she goes to practice.

"You didn't come to Logos," you say.

"Oh, sorry, I forgot," she says without looking at you. You're sure she's lying.

"Did you get everything straightened out with the teacher about your test?" you ask. You figure it's better to just get to the point.

"Yeah. I got it all straightened out. Don't worry about it," she says.

"What did he say?" you say, pushing a little.

"I said I took care of it!" she says with a disturbing scowl on her face.

With that she storms into the gym. *She didn't tell him*, you think. *And she's not going to.*

"I guess you've made your choice," you say aloud to the closed gym doors. "You're on your own now."

"Charlene is in detention," Karen announces to Logos one morning.

"Why?" Craig insists. "What did she do?"

"I don't know. All I know is that it's not the first time," Karen explains.

"Cheating again," Mark says. "I saw her detention slip when I was working in the office yesterday."

Karen groans. "How could we let this happen?" she says.

"We? It's not our fault!" Craig says. "We did everything we could to help her."

"Did we?" Karen asks. "I'm not so sure."

You stop going to Logos. What's the point? They all seem to be out to protect themselves there. Why bother? You find yourself alone more and more. Eventually Five Alive is a distant memory.

The End.

After only one month of meeting, the Logos Club has grown to over forty members. Five Alive acts as a steering committee and comes up with some rules.

"I think we should split this group up," C. J. suggests. "There's no way we can get to everyone's prayer requests or help them when they need it."

"Maybe we should just limit it to prayer time and pick prayers out of a hat to pray," Craig says.

"That wouldn't be fair," Karen says. "Besides, we're here to do more than pray. We're here to help one another live what we believe."

"Then I repeat, we need to split the group up," C. J. says.

It's decided that the club will be split in two, each meeting at the same time but in different rooms. Mr. Mac has to petition the administration for another room to use. They are reluctant, but Mr. Mac assures them he will monitor both rooms.

The next month everything seems to be going really well. You start to see some of the kids from Logos show up at your church.

Just when you think things couldn't get any better—the attack begins!

Red flyers covered with messages of evil intent start appearing in club members' lockers. Five Alive's lockers are spray painted to look like dripping blood. Mr. Mac calls an emergency meeting of the steering committee to discuss what's going on.

"This morning my classroom was trashed," he says. "The administration is not thrilled with this turn of events. Other teachers are concerned that their rooms might be next."

"Why would their rooms be targeted?" you ask.

"Because Ms. Kammer, the math teacher, and Mr. Ross, the language arts teacher, have both made it clear that they support Logos. They've even suggested to their students to try it out," Mr. Mac explains.

"Coach K isn't happy either," Charlene says. "Whoever it is spray-painted the gym bleachers with red paint last night."

"How are we supposed to do anything about this?" you ask. "We don't even know who is behind it all."

Even as you say that, you catch yourself wondering about Terry. Could Terry be behind any of this?

If you ignore the attacks, go to page 41.

If you start retaliating, go to page 43.

More people coming to Logos means more people hearing what you are struggling with. You worry that there won't be any confidentiality. The thought of dozens of people knowing what you worry about or what you've done wrong makes your skin crawl. *Why can't things just stay the way they are?*

That Friday at a steering committee, which is the five of you, meeting at your house, you tell everyone your concerns.

"We can't let just anyone join Logos," you say with authority. "Who knows what could happen?"

"What are you so worried about?" Karen asks. "God is doing great things in the lives of everyone we know. Why wouldn't we want that for everyone who is interested?"

You wonder when Karen was made king.

"It's too big," you insist. "How can we have deep conversations or deal with everyone's prayer requests in such a large group?"

"You've got a point," C. J. says.

"Thank you!" you say with relief.

"We can deal with that," Karen continues. "I think you're overreacting."

"I don't think I'm alone in this," you say, and nod to C. J. for agreement. "Why don't we vote on it?"

"Fine," Karen says. "All those in favor of allowing anyone who wants to join Logos join, raise your hand."

It's three to two. You lose.

If you accept the decision, go to page 37.
If you drop out, go to page 14.

The next week, hardly anyone shows up to the meeting. Both groups are combined back into one classroom. That same morning a special faculty meeting is held to discuss clubs on campus. Not only has Logos been attacked, but at the same time another group has petitioned to form a club on campus—a Ku Klux Klan club! During your meeting you all pray that their petition will be denied. You are horrified to think your school might allow such a club.

After the meeting Mr. Mac returns from the faculty meeting. "Well, I have some good news and some bad news," he says. "The good news is that the administration denied the KKK group from meeting."

"That's great!" C. J. says, and everyone starts cheering.

"But that's not all," Mr. Mac continues. "Logos can no longer meet here either."

The group is stunned into silence.

"Why? What did we do wrong?" Craig asks. "We're not the ones causing problems here."

"You haven't done anything wrong. But the administration has reconsidered in light of both the vandalism and the petition from the KKK group," Mr. Mac explains.

"I get it," Karen says. "If they're going to allow us to meet on campus, they have to allow anyone else who wants to, right?"

"Right," Mr. Mac says.

"Then we'll meet off campus," Craig suggests. "My house is closest to the school. We could meet there."

Everyone starts talking at once with renewed excitement. Together you decide not to let this decision get in your way. The next week more students than ever show up. Craig's mom goes out of her way to make kids feel welcome in their home. In fact, Mr. Mac and Mr. Ross show up to pray with the group every week.

Together the group decides to make an effort to visibly help at the school. Small groups commit to volunteer work, and your group is in charge of grounds beautification. Spring is in the air, and there's a lot of work to do outside almost every day after school.

It feels so good to be so involved, but in the back of your mind you know that you've let your studies take a back seat. An upcoming science test looms and you know you're not nearly ready, but you still don't take time to study. After all your work with Logos during the day, you want to just lounge in front of the TV at night.

The day of the test arrives. You're so nervous, you feel sick to your stomach. That gives you an idea: maybe you could stay home sick so you won't have to take the test.

If you go to school, go to page 77.

If you fake being sick, go to page 78.

"I think I know who is behind this," you say when Mr. Mac leaves—though you don't have any proof.

"How could you?" Craig asks.

"Call it intuition, but Terry has been pretty vocal to me about Logos," you say.

"Terry still talks to you?" Karen asks. "I thought you two were history."

You shrug.

"We need proof," Craig says. "Any idea how we can get some?"

"I can start hanging out with Terry again," you suggest. "I'll start showing up to play ball before school in the mornings."

"You'll miss Logos," Karen says, obviously disappointed.

"It's just temporary," you explain. "Just until I get proof."

"Then we can move into phase two," Craig says. "Payback."

"I'm not convinced this is the right thing to do," Karen says. "It feels wrong."

"Wrong? And what about what they've done to us? Isn't that wrong?" Craig insists.

Karen and a few others continue to speak warnings to you and Craig. You're sure they'll feel differently once you get proof.

It takes three weeks of playing basketball with Terry before you get what you need. At first Terry is suspicious of your sudden friendship, but you smooth things over quickly and Terry begins to trust you.

The day finally arrives when you have the proof. Five Alive joins you behind the field house after school to see. You flip open an old, moldy tarp to reveal a dozen cans of spray paint.

"This is the stash Terry told me about," you explain.

"Let's use their own weapons against them!" Craig yells as he grabs two cans of paint. You, Charlene, and C.J collect your own portions.

"Stop it," says Karen. "This is crazy!"

You all ignore her and sneak into the empty school, planning out your attack. Karen goes home.

You job is to point out all the lockers of Terry

and company. Craig and the others do the rest. Their artwork is inspiring! You all feel vindicated and free and go out for pizza to celebrate.

The next day there is a school-wide assembly. The principal and some of the teachers, including Mr. Mac, look somber as they take their seats in the auditorium. The recent vandalisms are the topic of the day.

"We've worked hard to build a strong community in this school," the principal says. "In less than a month that community has been destroyed."

"It's bad enough that whoever did this has no respect for school property," he continues. "It's the obvious fact that they have no respect for them-selves or others that grieves me and the rest of your teachers the most."

After an hour-long lecture, you feel horribly guilty. *Things just got out of hand,* you think. *It's not like we meant to hurt anyone.*

Someone pulls you aside out of the crowd of kids spilling out of the auditorium.

"Just tell me now so I can stop worrying," Mr. Mac says. "Tell me you and Logos weren't a part of any of this."

If you confess, go to page 89.
If you don't confess, go to page 48.

In your small group you confess that you faked being sick to avoid the science test. It is so scary to say it out loud, but Charlene is in your group. If anyone would understand, she would.

"I can hardly blame you for that," she says. "We've been way too busy to keep up with homework. But it still wasn't right."

"I know," you say. "And the sad thing is that I knew it at the time." You're quiet for a moment before you ask the question that is burning in your heart. "Does God forgive you when you do something wrong even though you know it's wrong?"

"God forgives us if we are honestly sorry," Mark says. "I think the tough part about doing something wrong while we're planning to ask for forgiveness later is that we're not really sorry."

"Are you sorry?" Charlene asks.

You don't say anything for a minute. "Yes," you finally say. And you mean it. "I am sorry that I cheated, but I don't know what else I could have done. I was desperate."

Nobody says anything for a moment. All this silence is painful.

"I think that I need to cut back on all the things we're doing with Logos so that I won't be tempted to do this again," you say.

You are so relieved that everyone agrees with you. And no one pushes you to confess to your teacher. But you are even more relieved that you don't have to feel guilty anymore. You wonder how God can possibly forgive so easily, but you are thankful he does.

That afternoon you discover a note in your locker.

Liar! is all it says. You quickly look around, but no one is looking in your direction. You're convinced Terry is the one being so hateful. But how would Terry know about your faking sick? Suddenly you know. If you were a cartoon character, a lightbulb would be hanging over your head. Billy joined Logos last month. Maybe he's not what he appears—someone who is interested in following Christ. Maybe he's a mole!

If you spend some time with God, go to page 50.

If you spend time worrying about Billy, go to page 51.

"I've got to go," you say and dash off.

Over the next few weeks attendance at Logos is down. Craig won't even talk about what happened. Karen, however, breaks the silence.

"I don't want to say I told you so," she says.

"Then don't," Craig says in annoyance.

"We've got to get past this," Karen insists. "Everything's falling apart."

"Then let it!" Craig jumps to his feet and slams his hands down on the desk.

Your mind races with how you could have done things differently. Retaliating seemed like the right thing to do at the time.

"Let's do what's right," Karen says. She's close to tears now. Craig doesn't usually lose his temper like that. "Let's confess and get it over with."

"Let's?" you say. "You didn't do anything."

"No, but I knew what you were going to do, and I didn't stop you. Come on. Let's do what's right."

Everyone else nods reluctantly in agreement. Before you can say anything, Mr. Mac walks in.

"Sorry to interrupt, but I've got bad news," he says. "Today is the last Logos meeting."

"Why?" Karen asks.

"The administration believes it has caused too much trouble. They've revoked their permission for you to meet," he explains. He sighs deeply and turns away from you. "It didn't have to be this way."

"What do you mean?" you ask.

He turns to look at you, looking into the eyes of each of you. "I'm disappointed that you decided to handle things yourselves instead of asking for help," Mr. Mac says.

Nobody says anything. You wonder how much he knows.

"What would you have done?" Craig asks, now sitting back down.

"I wouldn't have taken things in my own hands," Mr. Mac says. "Listen, even if you couldn't come to me for some reason, you could have gone to God with your problems."

Okay. He knew.

"Isn't that the whole point of this group?" he says, pressing further.

No one says anything.

"I am sad to say that I would no longer sponsor this group even if you were allowed to meet."

Logos disbands. Sometimes you pass former members in the hall and you eye each other with the knowledge of what once was.

The End.

You really don't know if Billy is a mole or not. You really don't know if Terry is behind all these attacks. You can only concentrate on what is real—what is true. That night you confess to God.

Heavenly Father, I know you see everything. You see the good and the bad in me. I can't hide from you. I don't even know why I try. Forgive me for lying to my mom and my teacher about being sick. I was scared. I knew I didn't do my part to prepare for that test. Help me now to do what is right. Help me to accept whatever consequences that come. Help me to remember to come to you first in any situation. Thank you for my friends. They love you and I feel so safe with them. Thank you for helping me to be who I say I am, even when it's hard. Amen.

You never find out if Billy joined Logos to spy, but you do see him become a Christian. Your mom throws a big party to celebrate. You know these are the best days of your life.

The End.

Your pillow is wet from your crying. Everyone must think you're an idiot. Logos was a dumb idea. You bare your soul only to have someone like Billy tell everyone in the world about it.

There's a soft tap at your bedroom door.

"Sweetie, are you alright in there?" your mom asks on the other side of the door.

You wipe your sleeve across your face and sit up straight in bed.

"I'm fine, Mom," you say. "Thanks."

"I'm here if you need me. Always," she says. And then at the last moment, "Goodnight, hon."

Always. Mom is always there for you. You let her down, too. You feel terrible all over again. You were supposed to study for your test, but now you don't care. You just want to cry.

The next Monday at Logos everyone looks different to you. Charlene is happy go lucky. How can she be after what she did? How can she just forget it all and act as if she never did anything wrong? You feel separate, no longer connected to the group.

"Here," she says and hands you a card.

Inside is a gift certificate to your favorite arcade. "What's this for?" you ask, stunned.

"My dad gave it to me for getting an A in science, but I don't need it," Charlene explains. "I knew you'd like it, so here it is!" Charlene is beaming. She's so happy to give it to you.

"But I didn't get an A in anything," you protest. "I don't deserve this."

"Doesn't matter," she insists. "All you have to do is take it and enjoy it."

Charlene waves goodbye and runs off to practice with her team.

The End.

"Aww, people are just jealous of us because we're so popular," C. J. says while stuffing his face with chips.

"Maybe it's more than jealousy. Maybe it's envy," Karen says.

"Uh, what's the difference?" Craig asks.

"Being jealous means wishing you have the good things others have. Being envious means wanting others to not have the good things they have," Karen explains. "I suspect that whoever called us is envious of us, for some reason. They want to break us up."

"Do you think we're too cliquish?" Charlene asks after a moment of silence. "I guess it's true that we hang out only with each other."

"But I only have eyes for you!" C. J. croons.

"Stop it, C. J.," Charlene says. "I'm serious. If I were someone outside of Five Alive, I'd think we were a closed club."

"We're not stopping anyone from joining us," you say.

"But we're not inviting anyone either," Karen says.

"Maybe it's time we thought about changing that," Craig says.

If you start brainstorming, go to page 15.

If you don't want to change, go to page 19.

The next Monday you go to Logos instead of playing ball with Terry. Your lifelong friendship with Karen and the others is worth giving it another try.

"Hey, stranger!" C. J. says as you walk into the room. Everyone looks up at you, and even kids you don't know smile at you.

"Welcome back," Mr. Mac says and shakes your hand. "This is a definite answer to prayer."

"We missed you," Karen says. "We all missed you."

Any fear you had previously disappears. "What do you mean an answer to prayer?" you ask.

"We've been praying for you since the first day of club," Charlene says. "We didn't know why you left, but we prayed that God would show you the right path."

You feel tears well up inside and fight to keep them hidden. *They prayed for me? Every week? Me?*

"Why don't we get started," Mr. Mac suggests. "Let's give our friend here a moment to catch up."

Karen opens the group in prayer and she thanks God for your safe return.

At the end of the meeting Five Alive hangs back to talk to you.

"I'm so sorry I was such an idiot," you begin. "The thought of living what I believe in front of everyone really scared me. I'm sorry if I let you all down."

"You didn't let us down," Charlene says. "But we're glad to have you back."

If you accept their forgiveness, go to page 37.

If you hate being imperfect, go to page 69.

Weeks go by, and life seems to go on without you with Five Alive. The Logos club is all they're interested in these days. No more hanging out at your house on Fridays for pizza and a movie. No more working on homework together. No more goofing around in the park on Saturdays. Logos has a life of its own. It has definitely replaced Five Alive. You just want your friends back. *Is that so wrong?*

One day you are shooting hoops with Terry. (You couldn't find Chris anywhere.) You notice your old friends walk by. "Quit staring at them!" Terry says and throws the ball at you before you're ready.

"Back off," you say.

"They're not worth your time or your staring," Terry says. "They dumped you, remember."

"Actually, I was the one who sort of dumped them," you say. This truth suddenly makes you sick inside. You look longingly at Charlene, Karen, C. J.,

and Craig as they enter the school deep in conversation. *That used to be me,* you think.

"Snap out of it!" Terry says. "Hey, I've got an idea of a way to get your mind off of those losers."

You follow Terry to the field house. Hidden underneath an old moldy tarp are a dozen different cans of spray paint.

"Where did these come from?" you ask.

"Coach uses them to mark the fields. They're here for the takin'," Terry declares proudly.

"Here," Terry says. "Let's finish this once and for all."

Terry tosses you a can a red spray paint and motions for you to follow to a window at the far end of the school. It turns out to be the classroom where Logos is meeting. You and Terry crouch beneath the window and wait.

"Lord, we remember our friend who is lost. We pray for your protection and guidance," Charlene prays aloud. You wonder if she's talking about you.

Terry snickers and rolls on the ground with muffled laughter. The bell rings and the classroom empties.

"We have two minutes," Terry says.

"To do what?" you ask naively.

"Watch and learn," Terry says and begins to spray the window.

Losers Club—Everyone Welcome!

The letters bleed down to the windowsill. You are horrified! Terry sticks the can in your hand. "Your turn," he says.

But before you can decide what to do, a voice bellows from behind. "May I help you two?" the voice asks.

Out of stupidity Terry answers without turning around, "No, we've got it under control."

"Really? Think again." It's Mr. Carlson, the school resource officer.

Busted!

That day in the principal's office you have a lot of time to think. At one point Charlene is working in the office and sneaks a note to you. It says, **Come back when you're ready. We miss you.**

I wish I could, you think.

If you go back to Logos, go to page 54.
If you don't go back, go to page 56.

"Charlene, you got a minute?" you ask during lunch.

"Sure. What's up?" she says.

"Let's go outside and talk," you say.

You wander around the patio area outside the lunchroom for a couple of minutes without saying a word.

"What's with you?" Charlene asks. "Why are you so moody all of a sudden?"

"I'm not moody," you say. "Just concerned."

"About what?" she asks.

"About you," you say. "I don't think the Logos Club is doing you any favors."

In what feels like a mad rush, you spill all of your worries to Charlene. "You confess, but then turn around and do the same thing the next day," you end. "It isn't right."

Charlene stares at you for a moment. "Who are you to judge me?" she finally explodes. "I thought you were my friend!"

"A friend tells you the truth," you say. "Even if it hurts."

"I don't need that kind of friend!" she says and then stomps back into the lunchroom.

If you hope that when she cools down, she will change her mind, go to page 64.

If you yell after her, go to page 74.

You never go back to Logos. You quit hanging out with Terry. Chris doesn't want anything to do with you. You remain alone and miserable.

The End.

The next morning you see Charlene at her locker right before English.

"Hey, Char, " you say.

"Hey!" she says.

You know you could talk to her now, but you keep quiet. Suddenly half the contents of her locker spill onto the floor. "Oh, no! I'm going to be late!"

You're kind of relieved by the distraction. You scramble to help her pick up her books and stuff them back into her locker. Then you both sail into English right before the bell.

"Thanks," she whispers to you. "I can't afford to be late in here again."

You can't help thinking that's not the only thing she should be worried about. *Maybe it'll all work out on its own*, you think.

The following Monday in Logos, Charlene says she has an announcement to make.

"Last week I really dropped a bomb on all of you. I'm very sorry," she says. "I see now that I really messed up—thanks to Mark."

Mark?

"It was nothin'," Mark says turning three shades of red.

"Mark confronted me and encouraged me to tell Mr. Ross that I cheated on his test. I was scared, but Mark came with me when I did," she explains.

"What happened?" Craig asks.

"I retook the test right then and there. I probably didn't do very well on it, but I feel a whole lot better," she says beaming at Mark. "I couldn't have done it without him."

"That's what friends are for," Mark says in the most humble of voices.

That is what friends are for, you think. *Why didn't I say anything?*

The End.

You're left wondering if you did the right thing. It was one of the hardest things you've ever had to do. You can't imagine never being friends with her.

Over the next couple of days you slip notes into her locker: "I'm here if you need me." "I miss you." "We can get through this, right?"

Finally, after a week of wooing, Charlene smiles at your most recent note: "Scream if you want, but please talk to me." She says, "I'm still mad at you." But she sits down next to you—and she's smiling.

"No, you're not," you say, smiling back. "You're so glad to have a friend like me."

She laughs, and then she grabs your arm. "You area great friend. I talked to Mr. Ross; he made me retake the test with penalty, but I can still play ball. Thanks for making me do the right thing."

"You would have done it, anyway," you say.

Charlene tells everyone at the next Logos meeting how you helped her to make the right choice by believing in her. "When someone believes the best you, you get a taste of being loved by God."

Charlene's excitement is contagious. It has suddenly become cool at your school to be a Christian. You're not surprised when she is nominated for student council president. But the best thing about being one her best friends is not that she is so popular, but that she always helps you to remember that you are loved by God.

The End.

"No, they don't," you say. "Actually, what I mean to say is—No, I don't hate you."

It took a second for Charlene to process what you just said, but then the horrified look in her eyes revealed her understanding of the situation.

"You? No way," she stutters. "Why would you? How could you?"

A fresh load of tears streams down her already streaked face. This feels like the worst day of your life. The final bell rings and you both see the principal searching the hallway for latecomers.

"I thought I was helping," you begin. "I thought—"

"I don't care what you thought. You thought wrong." Charlene brushes past you toward her first period class. You are left standing alone in the hallway. The principal zeroes in on you and you hesitate.

If you hope that when she cools down, she will forgive you, go to page 64.

If you holler back at her, go to page 74.

"Yeah." You hesitate. "That's pretty lousy."

Charlene opens her locker and peeks into the mirror mounted on the door.

"I look awful," she complains. "Stupid makeup." She pulls a tissue from her jacket pocket and carefully wipes the smeared mess around her eyes.

"No one believes me," she says.

"What do you mean?" you ask.

"I didn't have time to see Mr. Ross yesterday. I was already late for practice," she explains.

Suddenly you realize what Charlene is about to tell you. Already you feel like a total jerk.

"I had my test and everything. I was going to tell him and then beg for mercy," she says and then starts crying all over again. "Why would someone be so mean?"

"Maybe they weren't being mean," you suggest. "Maybe they were just being stupid." *That's an understatement!*

The next day you see Charlene talking with Five Alive. She's crying again. When you walk up, the four of them turn and look straight at you. No one looks happy. "Charlene's parents told her how Mr. Ross found out that she cheated," Karen announces.

"They did?" is all you can say.

"I thought you were my friend," Charlene sniffs as she breezes past you. It's the last time she ever speaks to you.

The End.

"Don't worry. I'm back. And you'll never have to forgive me again," you promise.

Today is the first day of the rest of your life! You feel focused and rejuvenated, like you could conquer the world. You are determined never again to be in a position where you'd have to confess. You are sure that you can always do the right thing if you try hard enough.

A few months later at a Logos meeting you are surprised when Charlene interrupts you. You had been telling one of the new kids how crazy he was to keep messing up. "It's so much better to just do the right thing," you were saying.

"Ummm," says Charlene, "being perfect is not all it's cracked up to be. I mean, some people—" you are sure she glances at you "—are so afraid of making mistakes that they drive everyone else crazy. Some people think being a Christian means being perfect. Actually, Christians are the same as everyone else, just forgiven."

"Yeah, but we don't want to do what you do,"

you say before you can stop yourself. Everyone is looking at you. "You know, keep confessing all the rotten things you do, but never stop doing them."

Charlene stares at you for a moment and then runs out of the room.

You shrug and turn back to the group. You are surprised when C. J. stands up. "Let's just quit for today," he says. "Let's go find Charlene." He doesn't look at you.

You can't help noticing that people stop sharing what's on their heart at Logos if you're there. They start to avoid you in the hallway. Even your friends don't confide in you anymore. You never figure out why.

The End.

Your hand sweats so much that you have to keep switching the phone from hand to hand.

"Hello, Charlene, it's—" The nasty click of Charlene hanging up hurts like a slap in the face.

You punch redial.

"Charlene—" Click again.

You wait two minutes and then try again.

"I'm sorry!" you yell into the phone before she can hang up.

"Who is this?" It's Charlene's mom.

"Mrs. Rush," you say. How embarrassing is this? "I need to talk to Charlene."

"She's not available," she says.

"I want to apologize," you say. "Please see if she'll come to the phone."

Her mom covers the receiver with her hand and you hear a muffled argument in the background.

"What?" an extremely annoyed voice asks.

"Charlene, I'm sorry. Please forgive me for fighting with you," you plead.

"And?" she asks.

"And … I want to be friends again?" you say, hoping it's the right answer.

"No. Are you sorry for anything else?" she asks.

You hesitate. "No," you say. "No, Charlene, I'm not. I know that's not what you want to hear, but I

can't sit by and watch a good friend mess up her life," you explain. There's silence on the other end. *Did she hang up?*

Then you hear her sniffles. She's crying.

"Don't cry," you say. "But if you have to, just don't go where anyone will see you. Those raccoon eyes will scare people away!"

She laughs a little and you know you've broken through. It's going to be okay.

It takes some time, but you and Charlene heal the wounds you both inflicted. You become her confidante, and she becomes yours. You tell each other everything, but you also expect each other to do the right thing. Who knew that telling the truth could be so liberating?

The End.

You grab Charlene by her backpack and pull her toward you.

"What are you so peeved about?" you ask. You're definitely mad now. "I'm not the one who cheated."

"And I'm not the one who narced on a friend," Charlene says with venom.

"Well, then maybe we're not friends," you shout.

"I was stupid to ever think we were," she yells.

Charlene pulls away from you and storms into her class.

"Is there a problem here?" the principal says as he escorts you by the arm to your own class.

"No problem at all," you say. "Not anymore."

The next days and weeks are like a bad dream that you can't wake up from. Charlene doesn't talk to you or even look at you unless it's with an icy stare. She spends more and more time with Mark, who has suddenly become her best buddy.

If you make the first step to work things out, go to page 71.

If you never talk to her again, go to page 75.

The next day Charlene serves her first of three detentions for cheating. She stops coming to Logos. She avoids everyone. Losing one of your oldest friends is bad enough. Watching her turn her back on everyone else is worse. Every week in Logos you all pray for her. It doesn't have to be this way. It's her choice.

Logos becomes more and more popular. Eventually you find yourself leading your own small group, which becomes popular as well. One day you notice Charlene outside your meeting place as if she's trying to decide whether or not to come in. She doesn't. You think she's gotten exactly what she deserves.

Days later you see Charlene talking to Terry and company out by the bike racks. You hesitate. This concerns you, but is it worth it to say anything to her?

"Hey, Charlene," you say as you walk toward the group. "How have you been?"

It's a pretty innocent question.

"What do you care?" she snaps.

"So, when did you two hook up?" You avoid her question and point to Terry who is smiling like a cat who just caught a helpless and defenseless bird.

"We've been hanging out in detention," Charlene says and moves closer to Terry.

"Oh," is all you can say. You feel like someone punched you in the gut. Charlene would never have gotten cozy with Terry if she hadn't ended up in detention. And she wouldn't have ended up in detention if … "Well," you finally say, "see you around."

"Not if I can help it," she says just before she walks away.

The End.

It's tempting to stay home, but you couldn't face Logos without telling them the truth. And then they'd probably talk you into admitting what you did. You decide you'd better do the right thing.

The test goes terribly. You are the last person in the room, and you still don't think you have all the answers figured out. Craig leaves just before you do, and he gives you a look that says he did just as badly as you did.

Time's up, and Mr. Mac takes the test from you. You join your friends at the lunch table a few minutes later. "That was terrible!" you say.

"It wasn't bad," Karen says. "All you had to do was memorize a bunch of charts. It's not like math where you have to figure everything out."

"Yeah, but who had time to study?" you complain.

"Not me," says Charlene.

"Me neither," you say. "I really like Logos—it's kept me from making bad choices a few times already—but do you think we're taking it too far?"

"What do you mean?" Karen asks. You can almost see her hair stand on edge.

You wonder if you should press the issue. You don't want to offend her—and you really don't want her to know that you can't keep up with her.

If you press on, go to page 79.

If you give up, go to page 80.

It was too easy. All you had to do was go downstairs and sit at the table without eating or saying anything.

"What's wrong, honey?" your mom asked.

"I feel lousy," you said, and then you coughed.

"You're worn out," she said. "I want you to go straight upstairs and go back to bed. And from now on you need to be in bed by ten o'clock."

So you got a whole extra day to study for the test; but now it is time to face Logos. If you tell them the truth, they'll probably try to get you to confess to a teacher or something. But you hate keeping a secret from them.

If you confess at Logos, go to page 46.

If you don't confess, go to page 91.

"What I mean is that I can't be so busy all the time. I need to have time for homework, but I also need some time to just relax—"

"But the stuff we do with Logos is important!" Karen almost shouts.

"True. But so is personal sanity." You feel like yelling, but you don't. "Seriously, Karen. Don't you think that we have to be wise with our time? I still want to do Logos—I told you I love it—but I think we should make time for other stuff, too. Namely, sleep."

"I have to agree," says C. J. "We don't all have as much energy as you do, Karen."

"I agree," says Charlene quietly. "If we want to stick with this, we can't be wearing ourselves out. I don't think that we're pleasing God when just try to be such good Christians. We please him when our hearts are right with him."

"Yeah," says Craig. "I don't even have time to go to church anymore."

Karen sighs deeply and then smiles a little. "All right, you slackers. I guess you're right. Sorry for pushing so hard."

The amazing thing is that as soon as Logos spends less time doing stuff, the group grows. You see more and more people come to Christ. And you feel happy, not tired.

The End.

"Never mind," you say. "I don't know why I said that."

You notice the other kids look down. You almost think they look disappointed, but you can't imagine that that is true. And Karen looks downright smug.

"No problem," she says. "I know it's hard to keep up with it all, but it's worth it."

You make a personal commitment to work harder to keep up with everything. Your mom is very impressed when she sees how well you're doing at everything, but you don't really care. You're just tired.

However, when the beautification project is done and Karen announces the next project Logos is about to begin, you can't handle it anymore. You blow up. "Forget it, Karen," you say. "I'm sick of this. I'm going home to watch TV."

A few other people agree and leave with you. You feel nothing but relief. Once in a while you miss Charlene and C. J. and Craig, but mostly you're just glad to have your life back. You often wonder why you ever considered being a Christian. It's just too much work. You never know the peace of God.

The End.

You avoid your friends. You make sure you're not at your locker between classes. You ride your bike to school instead of riding the bus. You don't answer the phone when they call. Inside you feel a little guilty, but there hasn't been another threatening phone call, and you've found time to hang with your new heartthrob Chris.

You may not be getting any flack for being a Christian or for faking your faith, but you're also not getting any compliments from your teachers, and you start to disappoint your mom over and over again.

Every time you think of your old friends, you shrug your shoulders. But inside you know you'll get a sore shoulder quicker than you'll get over your friends.

The End.

You find your friends having another heart-to-heart in the cafeteria. You plunk down beside them.

"Hey, look who's come back from the dead," C. J. says.

"What are we talking about?" you ask, hoping they'll catch on that you still consider yourself part of the group.

"We're still trying to figure out why that dope would call us fakes," Charlene explains. They all eye you carefully to see whether you'll leave.

"I've been thinking about that, too," you say. "Why don't you come over to my house sometime to talk about it in private?"

You're thrilled that they say yes.

"So," you say over the kitchen table a few days later, "why would they call us fakes?"

Go to page 53.

"No," you say. "I'll talk to her and see if she'll tell Mr. Ross herself."

"Do you want me to confront her with you?"

"No," you say without hesitation. "I don't think we should gang up on her. This is going to be tough enough for her as it is."

"Okay," says Mark. "I'll just pray."

You shrug, but inside you are kind of impressed. You wouldn't have even thought of that.

Go to page 24.

"I'm not telling anyone. Charlene asked us to keep a secret. I for one will honor that request," you say.

"I don't know," Mark continues. "If she doesn't tell her teacher, maybe I should."

"What are you talking about?" you say a little too loud. Some kids nearby look your way. "It's not your place. If you are Charlene's friend, you'll forgive her and move on."

"Fine. I'll leave it alone," he says. "Maybe she'll do the right thing anyway."

Mark's hopes are not realized. The next week at Logos Charlene confides that she gossiped about a teammate; the girl found out and is hurt.

"It's so liberating to be open with all of you," she says. "It's nice to be able to tell you the truth and still feel safe. Thanks, guys!"

After four more meetings it's obvious that Charlene is stuck in a bad pattern of behavior. She confesses what she's done, you all forgive her, but then she continues to do the same things over and over again. If she isn't changing her behavior, maybe it means she's not really sorry. After all, things aren't getting better, they're getting much worse.

If you tell her that you see a problem, go to page 60.

If you don't do anything about it, go to page 62.

For some reason, you don't believe Charlene. You doubt she will ever confess. You are concerned that she will get into the habit of cheating, so you decide to take things into your own hands.

Go to page 27.

For some reason, you don't believe Charlene. You doubt she will ever confess. You are concerned that she will get in the habit of cheating. You have no idea what to do. You decide to get some advice from someone who knows better than you do.

Just then, Mark walks up. "I'm going to report her," he says to you.

"Who? Charlene?" you ask.

"Who else?" he replies.

Go to page 31.

"I wonder who it was," you say. "I didn't recognize the voice, but if I had to guess, I'd say it was someone in the gang Terry hangs out with."

"Seriously?" asks Charlene.

"Yeah. Do you know what they did last week—"

"Who cares?" Karen says with exasperation. "We don't even know if it was them. The point is that we've offended someone."

"Why would anyone think we're faking it?" Craig asks.

"I'm not faking what I believe," C. J. says. "I'm not afraid to show who I am." He goes into the pantry and begins digging around for some more food.

"No," Charlene says. "He certainly doesn't."

You're quiet. It hasn't been easy for you to live what you believe. It's not that you go out of your way to do just the opposite; it's that you don't make a big deal about your faith. Honestly, you think your friends are taking this whole faith walk thing a bit too far. You were a Christian before they were, and you never worried about living as one like they do now. It's getting kind of embarrassing.

"Let's forget about this and get back to our cele-bration," Craig suggests. "We deserve a chance to just relax for awhile."

"I can't forget," Karen says. "If there are kids out there who think our faith is just an act, that's a problem."

"What are we supposed to do about it?" Craig says. "We can't make them believe us."

"We can at least make sure we're not being offensive in any way," Karen says. "I want kids to be interested in Christianity because of me, not turned off because of me."

You know Karen's right, but you're afraid of where this is going. How seriously do they want to take this whole faith thing, anyway?

If you're willing to hear more, go to page 53.
If you want to go on with life, go to page 19.

"Can we please go to your classroom?" you ask.

"Oh no," he says. But he leads you to his classroom.

You walk past Craig. He looks at you and seems to instantly know what's going on. "Go get the others," you say to him.

He nods his head. A few minutes later you're all behind closed doors in Mr. Mac's classroom.

"I'm sorry," you say right away. "We got carried away. It was really stupid, Mr. Mac. What can we do to make it up?"

Your teacher is silent for a moment, his head in his hands. "I was your sponsor," he says quietly.

Five Alive looks around at each other. You hadn't thought about how this would affect him.

"We'll go to the principal and tell him you had nothing to do with it," you say quickly. We'll clean it up. We'll take detention every day for the rest of this year—"

"I don't know what the consequences will be, but that is not what is concerning me. I was your sponsor. You should have come to me to help you out when things got too tough. You shouldn't have taken things into your own hands."

"We feel rotten," says Charlene. "We were supposed to be the Christian kids. What a joke."

"Listen," says Mr. Mac, "you still are Christian kids. Christians are the same as everyone else, just forgiven."

"What do you mean?" Charlene asks.

"Go home tonight and pray to God, begging for wisdom. Tell him how sorry you are. And then come here tomorrow forgiven, okay? I'm going to talk to the principal and see if I can get this worked out. But I need each of you to promise that by receiving this grace you are saying you will never do this kind of thing again."

You all spurt out words of affirmation.

"Are you sure you understand?" he says. "You are receiving a lot of grace, so you should also be extending a whole lot of grace to others when they do wrong things to you. Got it?"

You get it. And this lesson lasts you a lifetime.

The End.

At the next Logos meeting, when it's your turn to request prayer, you tell everyone that everything is alright. You wanted to have people pray for your French exam, but you don't think you have a right to go to God about something selfish when you won't even confess what you did.

Soon, you quit Logos altogether because you don't feel like you're getting anything from it anyway. You lose touch with Five Alive—and with God.

The End.

GₑT Real!

Life Issue: I want to be the kind of friend people can trust and rely on.

Spiritual Building Block: Trust

Do the following activities to gain your friends' confidence in your friendship:

Talk About It:
Answer the following questions in a journal:
Lately, have you been the kind of friend that you would want your friends to be to you? Have you been honest with them?

Have you stuck up for them when someone else was down on them?

Have you forgiven them for something they did that hurt you?

Have you taken time to listen to them or help them when they've asked?

Have you encouraged them to do the right thing in a difficult situation?

Have you prayed for them?

GET Real!

Life Issue: I want to be the kind of friend people can trust and rely on.

Spiritual Building Block: Trust

Do the following activities to gain your friends' confidence in your friendship:

Think About It:

Don't keep all of those great thoughts about your friends inside. Tell a friend you are proud she did great on a test you know she studied hard for.

Bake cookies or make a card or tape for a friend who helped you learn a new trick on your scooter or who waited after school for you on the day you had to clean the science lab.

When someone else tries to use words to take one of your friends down a notch, use your words to bring them right back up.

If someone begins to make fun of your friend's new braces, let that person know your friend has such a great smile, the braces just make it shinier.

God gave us the gift of speech. Use it to spread his love to others.

GET Real!

Life Issue: I want to be the kind of friend people can trust and rely on.

Spiritual Building Block: Trust

Do the following activities to gain your friends' confidence in your friendship:

Try It:

Try praying for one of your friends each night before you go to bed.

Pray that a friend might be able to mend a quarrel with another one of your friends, or that a pal might find peace in a challenging situation at home.

Pray that a friend will forgive you for something you did to them that you regret.

Pray for a friend to have courage to try something new or that they will start coming to church.

You'll find yourself finding answers to your own list of prayers by talking to God about your friends' issues. You'll also feel good inside knowing you're helping your friends in such a powerful way.

The Word at Work Around the World

What would you do if you wanted to share God's love with children on the streets of your city? That's the dilemma David C. Cook faced in 1870's Chicago. His answer was to create literature that would capture children's hearts.

Out of those humble beginnings grew a worldwide ministry that has used literature to proclaim God's love and disciple generation after generation. Cook Communications Ministries is committed to personal discipleship—to helping people of all ages learn God's Word, embrace his salvation, walk in his ways, and minister in his name.

Faith Kidz, RiverOak, Honor, Life Journey, Victor, NextGen . . . every time you purchase a book produced by Cook Communications Ministries, you not only meet a vital personal need in your life or in the life of someone you love, but you're also a part of ministering to José in Colombia, Humberto in Chile, Gousa in India, or Lidiane in Brazil. You help make it possible for a pastor in China, a child in Peru, or a mother in West Africa to enjoy a life-changing book. And because you helped, children and adults around the world are learning God's Word and walking in his ways.

Thank you for your partnership in helping to disciple the world. May God bless you with the power of his Word in your life.

For more information about our international ministries, visit www.ccmi.org.